Twinkle, twinkle, Little Star

and Other Nursery Rhyme Lullabies

Published by Bonney Press,
an imprint of Hinkler Books Pty Ltd
45–55 Fairchild Street
Heatherton Victoria 3202 Australia
www.hinkler.com.au

BONNEY
PRESS

© Hinkler Books Pty Ltd 2015

Illustrators: Steph Baxter, Sarah Coleman, Sarah Dennis, Nicolò Giacomin & Lucia Calfapeitra, Lauren Hom,
Lalalimola, Mick Marston, Jess Matthews, Chris Robertson, Marie Simpson, Alice Stevenson, Yulia Vysotskaya.

ISBN: 978 1 4889 2719 5

Printed and bound in China

Contents

Twinkle twinkle little star
How I wonder what you are
Up above the world so high

Like a diamond in the sky
Twinkle twinkle little star
How I wonder what you are

Hush-a-bye, don't you cry,
Go to sleep, little baby.
When you wake
You shall have
All the pretty little horses,
Black and bays, dapples and greys,
Coach and six white horses.

Hush-a-bye, don't you cry,
Go to sleep, little baby.
When you wake
You shall have cake
And all the pretty little horses.

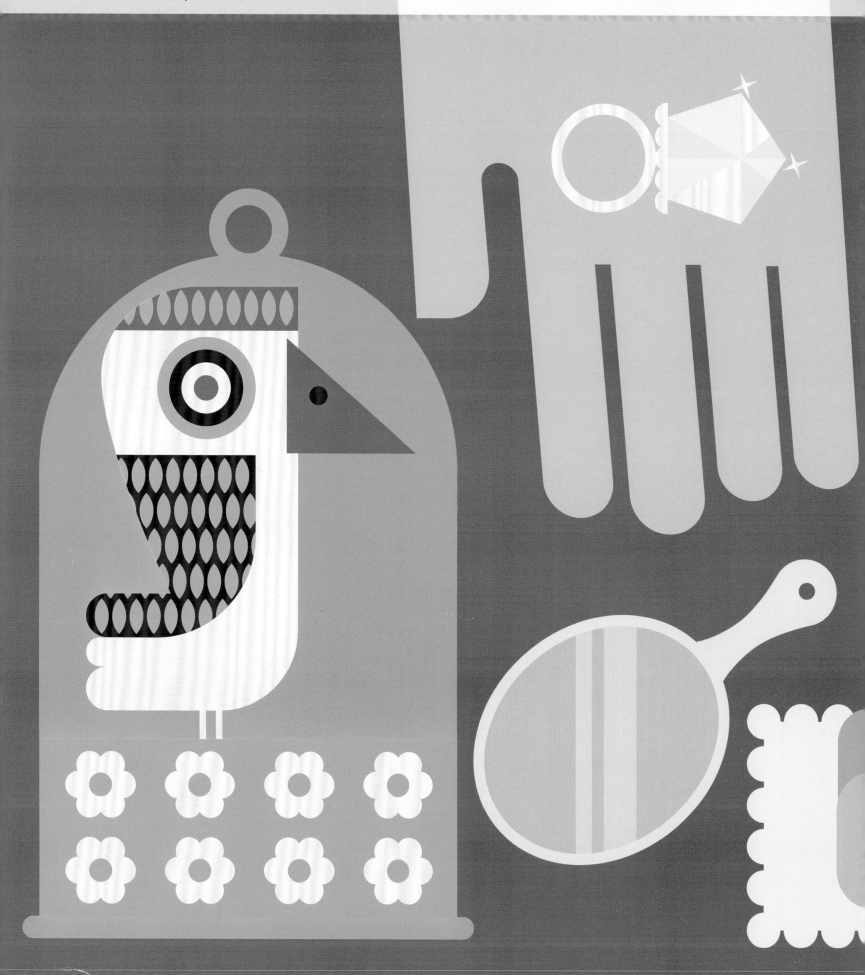

Hush, **little baby**, don't say a word,
Papa's going to buy you a mockingbird.

If that mockingbird won't sing,
Papa's going to buy you a diamond ring.

If that diamond ring turns brass,
Papa's going to buy you a looking glass.

If that looking glass gets broke,
Papa's going to buy you a billy goat.

If that billy goat won't pull,
Papa's going to buy you a cart and bull.

If that cart and bull turn over,
Papa's going to buy you a dog named Rover.

If that dog named Rover won't bark,
Papa's going to buy you a horse and cart.

If that horse and cart fall down,
You'll still be the sweetest little baby in town.

Day is done, gone the sun
From the lakes, from the hills, from the sky;
All is well, safely rest,
God is nigh.

Fading light dims the sight
And a star gems the sky, gleaming bright.
From afar, drawing near,
Falls the night.

Thanks and praise for our days,
'Neath the sun, 'neath the stars, 'neath the sky
As we go, this we know,
God is nigh.

Then good night, peaceful night,
Till the light of the dawn shineth bright;
God is near, do not fear,
Friend, good night.

Lullaby & goodnight,
With ROSES bestride,
With LILIES bedecked,
'Neath baby's SWEET BED.

May thou SLEEP, may thou REST,
May thy SLUMBER be BLEST,
May thou SLEEP, may thou REST,
May thy SLUMBER be BLEST.

Lullaby & goodnight,
Thy MOTHER'S delight.
Bright ANGELS around
My DARLING shall GUARD.

They will GUIDE thee from HARM,
Thou art SAFE in my ARMS.
They will GUIDE thee from HARM,
Thou art SAFE in my ARMS.

Frère Jacques,
Frère Jacques,
Dormez-vous?
Dormez-vous?
Sonnez les matines!
Sonnez les matines!
Ding, dang, dong!
Ding, dang, dong!

Are you sleeping,
Are you sleeping,
Brother John?
Brother John?
Morning bells are ringing!
Morning bells are ringing!
Ding, dang, dong!
Ding, dang, dong!

Sleep my child and peace attend thee, all through the night. Guardian angels God will send thee, all through the night. Soft the drowsy hours are creeping, hill and vale in slumber steeping, I my loving vigil keeping, all through the night.

WHILE THE moon HER WATCH IS KEEPING,
ALL THROUGH THE night
WHILE THE weary WORLD IS SLEEPING,
ALL THROUGH THE NIGHT.
O'ER THE SPIRIT gently STEALING,
Visions OF DELIGHT REVEALING,
BREATHES A PURE AND HOLY feeling
ALL THROUGH THE night

Little Boy Blue,
Come blow your horn,
The sheep's in the meadow,
The cow's in the corn.

Where is the boy
Who looks after the sheep?
He's under the haystack,
Fast asleep.

Will you wake him?
No, not I.
For if I do,
He's sure to cry.

Sleep, baby, sleep.
Thy father guards the sheep.
Thy mother shakes the dreamland tree.
And from it fall sweet dreams for thee.
Sleep, baby, sleep.

Sleep, baby, sleep,
Our cottage vale is deep.
The little lamb is on the green,
With woolly fleece so soft and clean.
Sleep, baby, sleep.

Sleep, baby, sleep,
Down where the woodbines creep.
Be always like the lamb so mild,
A kind and sweet and gentle child.
Sleep, baby, sleep.

star
light,
starbright, first star I see
tonight, I wish I may,
I wish I might,
have the wish
to night.
I wish

Golden Slumbers kiss your eyes,
Smiles await you when you rise.
Sleep, pretty baby, do not cry,
and I will sing a lullaby.

Cares you know not, therefore sleep,
while over you a watch I'll keep.
Sleep, pretty darling, do not cry,
and I will sing a lullaby.

Rock-a-bye, baby, on the tree top,
When the wind blows, the cradle will rock;
When the bough breaks, the cradle will fall,
Down will come baby, cradle and all.

I see the MOON;
The MOON sees me.
God bless the MOON,
And God bless me.

I see the stars;
The stars see me.
God bless the stars,
And God bless me.

I see the world;
The world sees me.
God bless the world,
And God bless me.

I know an angel
Watches over me.
God bless the angels,
And God bless me.

BYE, BABY bunting,
DADDY'S GONE A-HUNTING,
GONE TO GET A
RABBIT SKIN,
To wrap his BABY
BUNTING IN.